DRAWING TRICERATOPS
AND OTHER ARMORED DINOSAURS

STEVE BEAUMONT

New York

Published in 2010 by The Rosen Publishing Group, Inc.
29 East 21st Street, New York, NY 10010

Artwork and text: Steve Beaumont
Editor (Arcturus): Carron Brown
Designer: Steve Flight

Library of Congress Cataloging-in-Publication Data

Beaumont, Steve.
  Drawing Triceratops and other armored dinosaurs / Steve Beaumont. — 1st ed.
      p. cm. — (Drawing dinosaurs)
  Includes index.
  ISBN 978-1-61531-906-0 (library binding) — ISBN 978-1-4488-0432-0 (pbk.) —
ISBN 978-1-4488-0433-7 (6-pack)
  1. Dinosaurs in art—Juvenile literature. 2. Drawing—Technique—Juvenile literature.
3. Triceratops—Juvenile literature. I. Title.
  NC780.5.B395 2010
  743.6—dc22
                                       2009033250

Printed in China

CPSIA compliance information: Batch #AW0102PK : For further information contact Rosen Publishing, New York, New York at 1-800-237-9932

CONTENTS

INTRODUCTION...4

DRAWING TOOLS...5

DRAWING TIPS...7

TRICERATOPS...9

ANKYLOSAURUS...15

STEGOSAURUS...20

CREATING A SCENE...26

GLOSSARY...32

INDEX...32

WEB SITES...32

INTRODUCTION

"Dinosaurs"...the word conjures up all kinds of powerful and exciting images. From the three horns of Triceratops to the powerful clublike tail of Ankylosaurus and the dangerous tail spikes of Stegosaurus—dinosaurs came in all shapes and sizes.

These amazing creatures ruled Earth for over 160 million years until, suddenly, they all died out. No one has ever seen a living, moving, roaring dinosaur, but thanks to the research of paleontologists, who piece together dinosaur fossils, we now have a pretty good idea what many of them looked like.

Some were as big as huge buildings, others had enormous teeth, scaly skin, horns, claws, and body armor. Dinosaurs have played starring roles in books, on television, and in blockbuster movies, and now it's time for them to take center stage on your drawing pad!

In this book we've chosen three incredible meat-eating dinosaurs for you to learn how to draw. We've also included a dinosaur landscape for you to sketch, so you can really set the prehistoric scene for your drawings.

You'll find advice on the essential drawing tools you'll need to get started, tips on how to get the best results from your drawings, and easy-to-follow step-by-step instructions showing you how to draw each dinosaur. So, it's time to bring these extinct monsters back to life—let's draw some dinosaurs!

DRAWING TOOLS

Let's start with the essential drawing tools you'll need to create awesome illustrations. Build up your collection as your drawing skills improve.

LAYOUT PAPER

Artists, both as professionals and as students, rarely produce their first practice sketches on their best quality art paper. It's a good idea to buy some inexpensive plain letter-size paper from a stationery store for all of your practice sketches. Buy the least expensive kind.

Most professional illustrators use cheaper paper for basic layouts and practice sketches before they get to the more serious task of producing a masterpiece on more costly material.

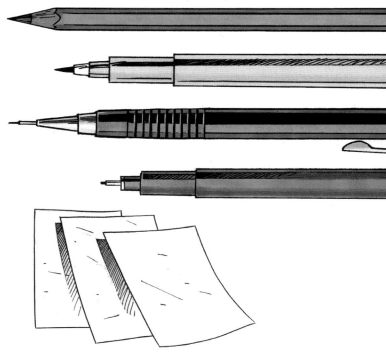

HEAVY DRAWING PAPER

This paper is ideal for your final version. You don't have to buy the most expensive brand—most decent arts and crafts stores will stock their own brand or another lower-priced brand and unless you're thinking of turning professional, these will work fine.

WATERCOLOR PAPER

This paper is made from 100 percent cotton and is much higher quality than wood-based papers. Most arts and crafts stores will stock a large range of weights and sizes—140 pounds per ream (300 g/sq m) will be fine.

LINE ART PAPER

If you want to practice black and white ink drawing, line art paper enables you to produce a nice clear crisp line. You'll get better results than you would on heavier paper as it has a much smoother surface.

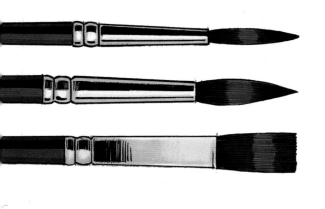

PENCILS

It's best not to cut corners on quality here. Get a good range of graphite (lead) pencils ranging from soft (#1) to hard (#4).

Hard lead lasts longer and leaves less graphite on the paper. Soft lead leaves more lead on the paper and wears down more quickly. Every artist has his personal preference, but #2.5 pencils are a good medium grade to start out with until you find your own favorite.

Spend some time drawing with each grade of pencil and get used to their different qualities. Another good product to try is the clutch, or mechanical pencil. These are available in a range of lead thicknesses, 0.5mm being a good medium size. These pencils are very good for fine detail work.

PENS

There is a large range of good quality pens on the market and all will do a decent job of inking. It's important to experiment with a range of different pens to determine which you find most comfortable to work with.

You may find that you end up using a combination of pens to produce your finished piece of artwork. Remember to use a pen that has waterproof ink if you want to color your illustration with a watercolor or ink wash.

It's a good idea to use one of these—there's nothing worse than having your nicely inked drawing ruined by an accidental drop of water!

BRUSHES

Some artists like to use a fine brush for inking linework. This takes a bit more practice and patience to master, but the results can be very satisfying. If you want to try your hand at brushwork, you will definitely need to get some good-quality sable brushes.

ERASER

There are three main types of erasers: rubber, plastic, and putty. Try all three to see which kind you prefer.

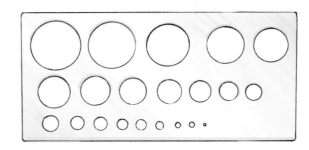

PANTONE MARKERS

These are very versatile pens and with practice can give pleasing results.

INKS

With the rise of computers and digital illustration, materials such as inks have become a bit obscure, so you may have to look harder for these, but most good arts and crafts stores should stock them.

WATERCOLORS AND GOUACHE

Most art stores will stock a wide range of these products, from professional to student quality.

CIRCLE TEMPLATE

This is very useful for drawing small circles.

FRENCH CURVES

These are available in a few shapes and sizes and are useful for drawing curves.

COLORING

After inking comes the final coloring stage. In this section we are going to go through the stages of coloring a Stegosaurus. The methods described are suitable for watercolors or colored marker pens. You could also experiment with colored pencils to achieve a similar effect.

STEP 1

Start by applying the base color. For Stegosaurus, a light sand color has been used. Notice how the color isn't completely flat and has texture to it. This can be achieved in the following ways: if you are using watercolors, try not to lay the color down too flatly or allow it to dry unevenly, looking slightly patchy. If you are using colored markers, wait until the first layer of ink has dried and then go over it using a blender marker. This will disperse the pigment in the ink for a textured effect.

STEP 2

Now apply light green to the back, neck, tail, and down the sides of the legs. If you're using watercolors, go over the top of the base color, keeping your strokes patchy and light. A good trick if you are using colored markers is to apply ink onto a cotton ball or tissue paper and quickly dab it onto the paper. This will create a nice uneven skin texture.

STEP 3

Now apply a light gray wash to the overall image to dull the colors. Add olive green to finish off the skin. Start to color the armored plates on its back in a yellowish orange color.

STEP 4

Using a darker orange of a similar tone, add shading to the darker areas of the armored plates. Finally apply some midrange gray to the skin where the folds and creases are and to the spikes protruding from its tail.

TRICERATOPS

DINO FACT FILE

Triceratops is most famous for its big three-horned face, which is exactly what its name means. This sturdy plant eater was like a modern-day rhino and would charge at its predators. Its most effective piece of armor was its big neck frill—a pointed, bony plate tipped with smaller plates. It also had very thick bumpy skin. All of this body armor was needed—T. rex was one of its predators.

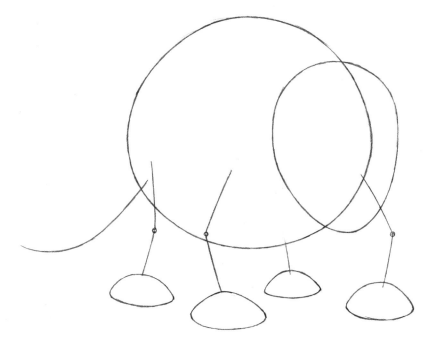

STEP 1

Start with the basic stick figure. At this angle the body is almost circular rather than egg-shaped.

STEP 2

Add the basic construction shapes. Note that the leg cylinders are much wider and stumpier than those of taller dinosaurs.

STEP 3

Now draw in the head and face. The mouth is shaped like a beak. When drawing this, slightly extend from the face oval. To create Triceratops's armored head crest, draw a sweeping arc on top of the oval. Now add the skin around the construction shapes.

STEP 4

Add the horns and toes and remove all of your unwanted lines and shapes.

STEP 5

Add details like bumps, creases, and wrinkles to the skin, and refine the shape of the legs. Add the first shading around the eye area.

STEP 6
Now finish the pencil drawing by shading in the dark areas to add depth. Add extra detail to the horns, plates, beak, and skin.

DID YOU KNOW?

TRICERATOPS HAD A HUGE SKULL. IT WAS 10 FEET (3 M) LONG. IT'S ONE OF THE LARGEST SKULLS OF ANY LAND ANIMAL EVER DISCOVERED.

STEP 7
Next ink over the pencil work.

STEP 8

Color the Triceratops using a sand-colored base for its skin. Add a pale olive green along its back, tail, and face. Then, using a midrange gray, add patchy shading to its legs and underbelly, around the eyes, and to the horns.

ANKYLOSAURUS

DINO FACT FILE

Ankylosaurus was a huge plant eater with very impressive body armor. Its whole top side was covered in thick oval-shaped plates and sharp spikes. It had a powerful clublike tail and even its eyes had special protective eye plates. The only way to hurt it was by flipping it over, exposing its soft belly. It's thought to have been fairly fast on its feet, but, like Stegosaurus, it had a tiny brain.

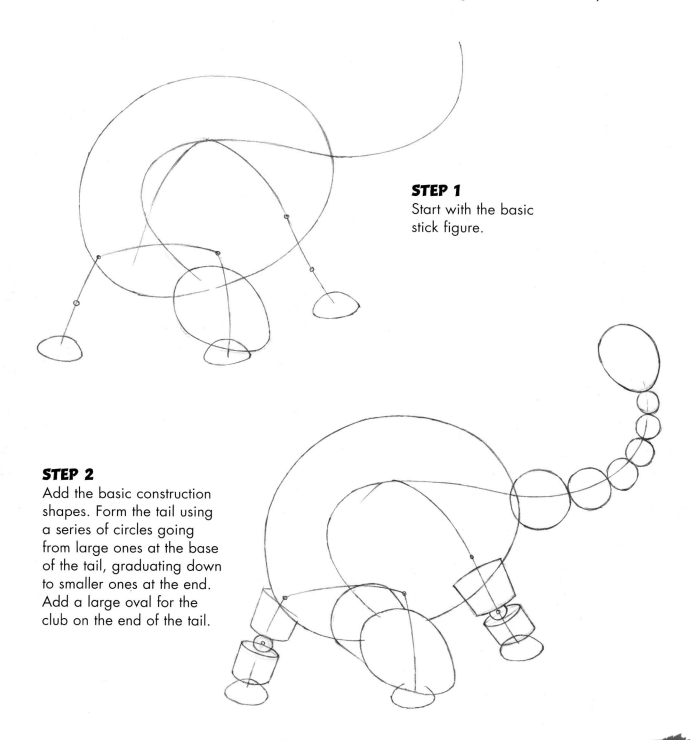

STEP 1

Start with the basic stick figure.

STEP 2

Add the basic construction shapes. Form the tail using a series of circles going from large ones at the base of the tail, graduating down to smaller ones at the end. Add a large oval for the club on the end of the tail.

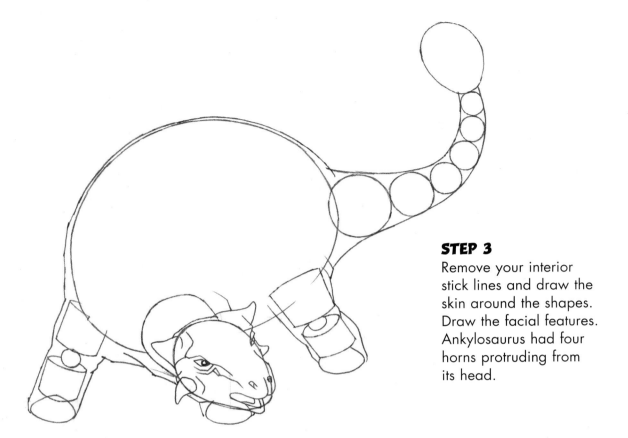

STEP 3

Remove your interior stick lines and draw the skin around the shapes. Draw the facial features. Ankylosaurus had four horns protruding from its head.

STEP 4

Erase your construction shapes. Add the claws on its feet and give definition to the skin with lines and creases. Now draw its armor plates. Start each one as an elongated oval with a central line. Then refine each plate using uneven lines to give them a realistic appearance.

STEP 5

Finish the pencil drawing off by adding shading. Notice how the shading on the armor plates gives added perspective. Finalize the face and club tail and remove any unwanted lines.

DID YOU KNOW?
ANKYLOSAURUS HAD A MASSIVE GUT TO PROCESS ALL THE FOOD IT ATE. SCIENTISTS THINK IT MUST HAVE PRODUCED LOTS OF WASTE GAS.

STEP 6

Ink over your final pencil work for a dramatic effect.

STEP 7

Color the Ankylosaurus starting with a light gray base for the skin color. Next apply a midrange gray over the top, leaving areas of the light gray visible around the underbelly and tail. Go over the back and the top of the head with dark gray. Use a light cream color for all of its armor—plates, horns, and claws.

STEGOSAURUS

DINO FACT FILE

Stegosaurus was a plant eater with an intimidating appearance. It was as big as a bus and had plenty of defense mechanisms on its body, starting with 17 bony plates running along its back in two rows. These plates continued down its tail, which it could swing around to defend itself and at its tip were sharp pointed spikes. All of its armor made up for its lack of teeth and tiny brain.

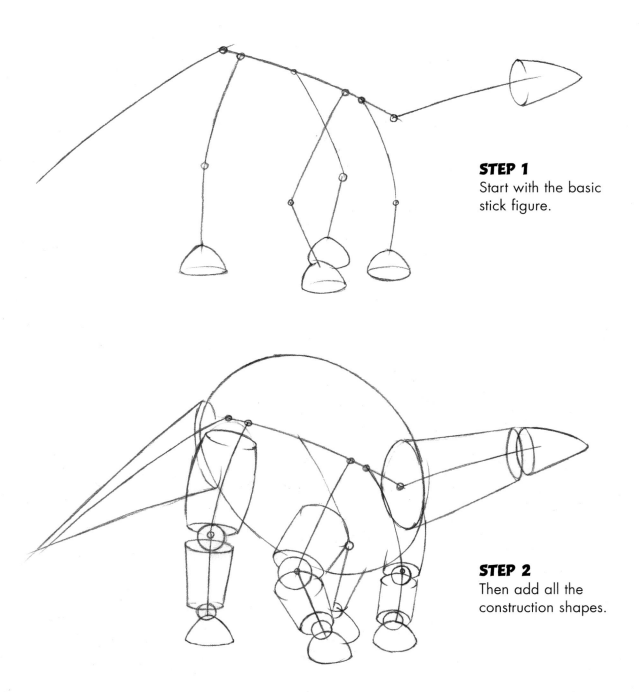

STEP 1
Start with the basic stick figure.

STEP 2
Then add all the construction shapes.

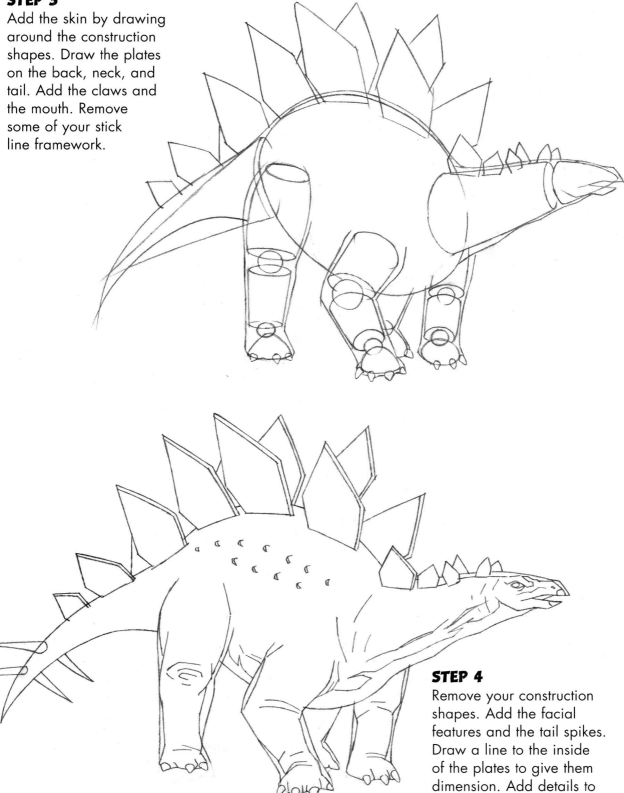

STEP 3

Add the skin by drawing around the construction shapes. Draw the plates on the back, neck, and tail. Add the claws and the mouth. Remove some of your stick line framework.

STEP 4

Remove your construction shapes. Add the facial features and the tail spikes. Draw a line to the inside of the plates to give them dimension. Add details to the arms, legs, and skin.

STEP 5
Finish the pencil drawing by adding details to the plates and skin, and add some shading.

STEP 6
Ink over the finished
pencil drawing.

STEP 7

Color the Stegosaurus using a sand-colored base. For the next layer, use a very pale gray. On top of the gray, apply a pale olive green, leaving areas of the sand color untouched around the underbelly and under the neck and tail. Using a dark olive green add texture to the skin along the back. Color the armored plates on its back using yellow and orange. See pages 7–8 for a step-by-step guide to coloring the Stegosaurus.

DID YOU KNOW?
STEGOSAURUS HAD ALL THAT FIERCE ARMOR FOR A REASON—ITS BRAIN WAS ONLY ABOUT THE SIZE OF A WALNUT!

CREATING A SCENE

LANDSCAPE FEATURING TRICERATOPS

Triceratops lived about 65 million years ago. This was the golden age of dinosaurs, just before their mass extinction. Many incredible creatures had evolved and this diversity was also found in the plants, flowers, and landscapes on Earth. Triceratops roamed the plains and valleys of what is now North America, where it grazed on low-lying plants.

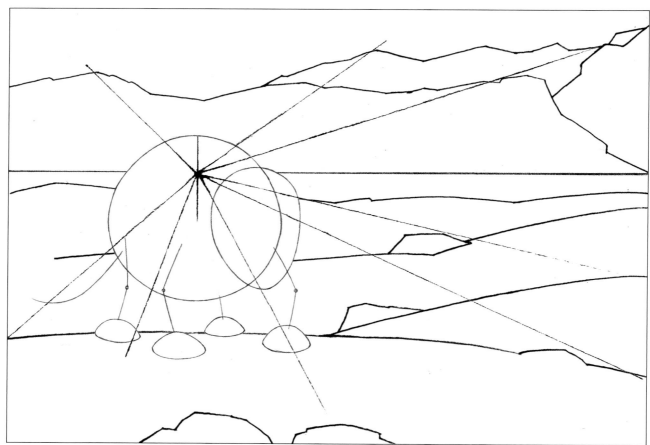

STEP 1 Draw the horizon line just above the halfway point on the page. Sketch in a line of craggy hilltops above the horizon line. Draw the stick figure for a Triceratops. Add a few lines to indicate an uneven surface across the desert plain and sketch a few rocks around the dinosaur.

STEP 2 Construct the Triceratops (see pages 9–14 for the step-by-step guide). Next, draw some fern-like plants in the foreground and develop the mountain rock.

STEP 3 Work pencil detail around the ferns, adding more plants if you like. Add clouds in the sky. Draw the neck frill, eyes, and beak onto the Triceratops.

STEP 4 Complete the pencil drawing by adding shading to create areas of black and all your final details to the dinosaur and scenery.

STEP 5 Finally, color your prehistoric landscape. You could experiment with other colors to create different effects.

GLOSSARY

cylinders (SIH-len-derz) Shapes with straight sides and circular ends of equal size.

facial (FAY-shul) Of the face.

gouache (GWAHSH) A mixture of nontransparent watercolor paint and gum.

mechanical pencil (mih-KA-nih-kul PENT-sul) A pencil with replaceable lead that may be advanced as needed.

perspective (per-SPEK-tiv) In drawing, changing the relative size and appearance of objects to allow for the effects of distance.

sable brushes (SAY-bel BRUSH-ez) Artists' brushes made with the hairs of a sable, a small mammal from northern Asia.

spikes (SPYKS) Sharp, pointy things shaped like a spear or a needle.

stick figure (STIK FIH-gyur) A simple drawing of a creature with single lines for the head, neck, body, legs, and tail.

tone (TOHN) Any of the possible shades of a particular color.

watercolor (WAH-ter-kuh-ler) Paint made by mixing pigments (substances that give something its color) with water.

INDEX

A
Ankylosaurus, 4, 15–19

C
claws, 4, 19

E
Earth, 4, 26

F
facial features, 16, 21

H
horns, 4, 10, 12, 14, 16, 19

S
shape(s), 4, 6, 9–11, 16, 20–21
sizes, 4–5
skin, 4, 8–12, 14, 16, 21–22, 24

spikes, 4, 8, 15, 20–21
Stegosaurus, 4, 7–8, 20–24
stick figure, 9, 15, 20

T
tail, 4, 7–8, 14–15, 17, 19–20, 24
teeth, 4, 20

W
watercolors, 6–7

WEB SITES

Due to the changing nature of Internet links, PowerKids Press has developed an online list of Web sites related to the subject of this book. This site is updated regularly. Please use this link to access the list:
www.powerkidslinks.com/ddino/triceratops/